Brownie Badges round the world

PAKISTAN

SWEDEN

COLUMBIA

JAPAN

FRANCE

ITALY

DENMARK

UNITED STATES OF AMERICA

AUSTRALIA

NIGERIA

A Brownie Guide is a member of the Girl Guides Association. She is between the ages of seven and eleven years.

The Girl Guides Association has members in over ninety countries. Anyone can belong: it doesn't matter if a girl is handicapped, what colour her skin is, or where she lives – provided she is willing to make the Threefold Promise, she can be a Brownie Guide. Even on big sheep farms in the far outback of Australia, a long way from a town, there are Brownies; they have their Pack Meetings by radio and post, just as they do their schooling.

A Brownie is a very busy and happy girl because there are so many new and interesting things to do when she becomes a Brownie. She makes many new friends, and with these friends finds out how to use her time in the most enjoyable and helpful way.

The Brownie Motto is 'Lend a Hand' and through all the exciting things she learns to do while a Brownie she discovers how best to carry out this Motto and live up to the important Threefold Promise she has made. You can read more about these later in the book.

BROWNIE GUIDES

by NANCY SCOTT

photographs by JOHN MOYES

illustrations by BERNARD ROBINSON
and ERIC WINTER

Ladybird Books Ltd
Loughborough 1978

"Quick! Let's hide behind here," and Mabel pulled her friend, Florence, behind a thick laurel bush growing against the garden wall. "They'll never see us here, and we'll see everything they do at their meeting."

"It would be much better if we could join them," grumbled Florence. "It's mean that they can have so much fun, and we can't, just because we're not eleven yet."

Who were Florence and Mabel talking about?

Well, if you are a Brownie Guide you will already have guessed. They were of course talking about their older sisters who had just joined the then new Youth Movement called The Girl Guides. This was in 1913, and the Girl Guide Movement had been growing bigger and bigger since the first Companies were started in 1910. The older girls were having a splendid time, so it wasn't surprising that Mabel and Florence wanted to watch them, and wanted even more to join in.

You see, at the beginning of the 20th century, girls were expected to stay at home and learn such useful, but ordinary, things as hemming and mending sheets and curtains, cooking daily meals, arranging flowers, cleaning and dusting. They weren't expected to do exciting things out-of-doors as their brothers did. In fact any girl who tried to do jolly things outdoors, like the boys, was called a tomboy or a hoyden, and older people frowned on them disapprovingly. Of course they were allowed to

go for walks, but even then they had to be ladylike.

Then something surprising happened which changed everything for many girls, and in time changed the thinking of many grown-ups about things that girls could, and should, do.

A new Youth Movement was started, at first just for boys. It was called Scouting, and was based on a book *Aids to Scouting* written by Robert Baden-Powell. He was an officer in the British Army, and because of his wise leadership he became a national hero in Britain.

Aids to Scouting was intended to help to train young soldiers, but boys and girls liked the exciting and interesting things in it, too. Soon groups of boys were meeting together and practising some of the new Scouting ideas. They called themselves Boy Scouts.

This surprised and pleased Baden-Powell so much that he decided to rewrite the book specially for boys. But first he wanted to try out some of his ideas with boys themselves, and see if the boys really enjoyed doing them.

To do this Baden-Powell arranged the first Scout Camp. This was in 1907 and in those days people didn't go camping and caravanning as they do today, so this was something quite new and exciting. The boys were a mixed group – some came from factories, some from Public Schools; some from poor homes, and some from rich ones, but they got on splendidly together and had a wonderful time. They cooked on fires out-of-doors, slept in tents, learnt how to track in open country, went swimming and hiking, and played exciting stalking and outdoor games. In the evenings they sat round a glowing Camp Fire while Baden-Powell told them grand stories about his adventures.

When the Camp was over, Baden-Powell finished his book, *Scouting for Boys*, and from this book has grown the Scout and Guide Movements as we know them today.

Baden-Powell intended his Scouting ideas for boys only, but girls didn't see why the boys should have all the fun. They wanted to be Scouts too. So all over the country groups of girls got together and called themselves Girl Scouts. In fact by November 1909, 6,000 girls had registered as GIRL SCOUTS at the new Scout Headquarters in London, and there must have been hundreds more all over the country not so registered.

When Baden-Powell realised that the girls not only wanted to be, but meant to be, Scouts, he set to work to organise a girls' Movement. He changed their name to Girl Guides, naming them after the famous corps of Guides in India who were then well known for their keenness, courage and general handiness.

It was a Patrol of these Girl Guides that Mabel and Florence were watching so enviously one Saturday morning in June. They were in Mabel's garden where the Girl Guides' Meeting was to be held. Mabel's sister, Merle, was a Patrol Leader.

All the Patrols had names. Once this Patrol had been called the Lions: that was when they had first started and called themselves Girl Scouts, just like the boys. But when they became Girl Guides, they changed their Patrol names, too. Now the Lion Patrol was called the Heather Patrol.

"Here they come," whispered Mabel, and squeezed her friend's arm excitedly.

Along the path leading to the bottom of the big garden marched eight girls, led by Merle.

"Oh my, don't they look splendid," sighed Florence enviously.

Yes, those early Girl Guides did look splendid in their smart uniforms of navy blue blouses, and navy blue skirts which scarcely reached their ankles. Wide-brimmed khaki Scout hats were set jauntily and proudly on their erect heads. The Girl Guides then much preferred the original Scout hats to the smaller hats the new Girl Guides were supposed to wear.

Every member of the Patrol also wore a white haversack over one shoulder, and on the haversack was a big Red Cross. These haversacks were filled with first aid items they might need – bandages, slings, splints, and safety pins. And every Patrol member carried a pole. Poles had many uses – they could be used to vault over streams and ditches; to make stretchers or to hold back a crowd from the scene of an accident. All Girl Guides and Boy Scouts carried poles in those days.

"What are they going to do today?" asked Florence.

"They're going to pretend that the stable is a house on fire, and they're going to practise different ways of rescuing people. Then they're going to cook their dinner over an open fire, and Merle is going to teach them how to make jam dampers."

"Oh, the lucky things! How exciting. It's not fair, why can't we be Girl Guides, too? We could rescue people and cook on fires, just as well as they can, I'm sure."

All over the country little girls under eleven years were saying the same thing as Florence – "Why can't we be Girl Guides?"

They wanted to wear a splendid uniform, and prove themselves as brave and helpful as their older sisters.

Again and again groups of under-elevens turned up at Girl Guide Meetings asking to join. Sometimes they were allowed to stay and watch, but of course the things the big girls did were usually much too difficult, even dangerous for little girls to do.

Not only that, but most of the Girl Guide Meetings in those days were held out of doors and often lasted the

whole day. So they weren't at all suitable for little girls who tired much more quickly than the older girls.

But still the under-elevens went on asking and asking, until at last the grown-ups realised they would have to do something for them.

And so the Rosebuds were started.

The idea behind the name 'Rosebud' was that a rose-bud grows and opens up into a rose eventually, and so it would be with these little girls, who would grow up and become Girl Guides one day.

Florence and Mabel, and other little girls of their age, were delighted to have meetings of their own at last, and begin to learn important and interesting things as their big sisters did.

They liked their uniforms, too. They were almost as smart as the big girls' uniforms – navy blue tunics and knitted caps or rush

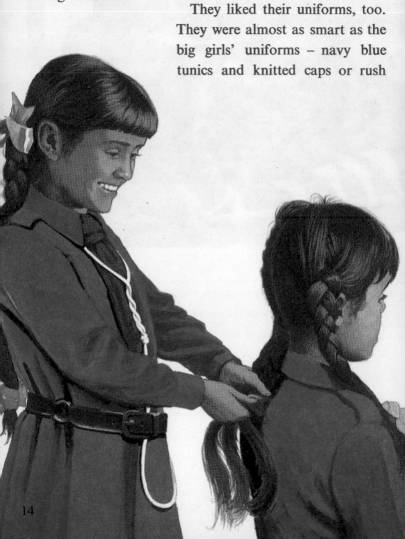

hats, brown belt and tie. Most groups had a rosebud as their badge, although some had acorns. Then they had various tests of skill and when they reached Second Class standard they gained a badge showing an acorn with leaves. When they became even more skilful they became First Class Rosebuds and added a motto to their Acorn badge.

Some of the things these Rosebuds learnt to do were much the same as Brownie Guides do today – such things as learning to lay a table; tie up a parcel firmly for posting; bandaging a cut finger. But some of the things they learned how to do would be of little use to Brownies today. Rosebuds learnt how to clean knives, forks and spoons, because people couldn't buy stainless ones then as they can now.

They also learnt how to plait their own hair. Girls of all ages at that time had really long hair, and it was the fashion for schoolgirls to wear it in plaits. So a Rosebud who could plait her own hair in the mornings was a great help to a busy mother.

But although they liked having their own Meetings at last, with their own exciting work and games – they didn't like their name! It didn't sound lively enough.

No, they didn't want to be Rosebuds. It was Guides they wanted to be!

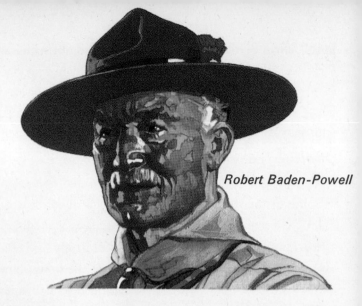

Robert Baden-Powell

However the Leaders of the Girl Guides felt that it wasn't right to call them Junior Girl Guides. But if they didn't want to be called Rosebuds, what were they to be called? All sorts of names were suggested, like Bees, Skylarks, Bantams, Buds.

But none of them suited the energetic busy younger girls.

It was the Founder of the Scout and Guide Movements, Robert Baden-Powell, who thought of just the right name – Brownies.

He said that people once believed there really were brownie folk who came secretly into homes where help was needed, and did all kinds of useful jobs and surprise 'good turns'. So he thought that Brownies was the name which would be just right for the helpful, happy little people the Rosebuds had proved themselves to be.

He was right. Brownies they became, and from only a few Rosebuds, their numbers grew and grew from hundreds to thousands. Then children in other countries heard about Brownies, and they too wanted to join in the fun. So from thousands it grew into hundreds of thousands, all over the world.

Not all of them are called Brownies, but you will read why that is later in the book.

When the Rosebuds became Brownies, they also made other changes. Not all at once, but gradually over the years.

The whole Pack then, as now, was divided into Sixes, just as a Guide Company and Scout Troop is made up of Patrols, which are small groups within a larger one.

Well, the Rosebuds and early Brownie Sixes were named after trees; but one day someone decided that as the Pack was named after the Brownie of English Folk Lore, it would be nice to have the Sixes named in the same way. So now the Brownie Six Names are: Gnomes, Pixies, Imps, Elves, Sprites, Irish Leprechauns, Scottish Kelpies, and Ghillie Dhus, or Welsh Bwbachods.

Gradually the uniform changed, too. The first Rosebuds wore blue, rather like the Girl Guides, but in time this was changed to a brown dress. The first Brownies wore hats, big straw ones in summer. These were later changed to woolly caps.

When a girl first joins Brownie Guides, the first thing she asks is – "Why are we called Brownies?"

The Brownie Guider – that is the name given to the adult Leader of the Pack – will then tell her *The Story of the Brownies*, which was originally written by Juliana Horatia Ewing.

A Brownie Guider talking to new recruits

The Story of the Brownies tells the story of Tommy and Betty who lived in a cottage on the edge of the woods. They were lazy, untidy, noisy and selfish. Their mother loved them very much, as all mothers do, but some days she became very weary indeed having to correct them over and over again.

One day they were particularly naughty. They had been playing a rough noisy game, they'd broken a cup and plate, they'd made their clothes very dirty; in fact they'd been a thorough nuisance, and their mother was very, very tired.

You see, as long as they had a good time they never thought what a worry they were to other people.

"Oh dear," sighed their mother, "how different things were when we had a brownie in the house."

"What is a brownie?' asked Tommy and Betty.

Their mother explained that the brownie was a little creature who came into the house before anyone was up, and cleaned and tidied up, and did all manner of useful jobs about the house and garden. She said he made everyone happy, but no one ever saw him because he always slipped away before anyone was up.

Tommy and Betty thought what a splendid thing it would be to have a brownie in their house, then they wouldn't have to do any jobs at all!

"Do tell us how we can find a brownie," they said.

"There's only one person who can tell you that," said their mother, "and that is the wise brown owl in the woods; she knows all about brownies."

The Owl was able to help them, but how they found her, and what she said to them and told them to do, you must find out for yourself. You can do this by asking a Brownie Guide to tell you the rest of the story, or by reading it in the Brownie Guide Handbook, or by becoming a Brownie yourself.

But this *can* be told – they found out that they themselves could become brownies, and once they had started being brownies they had such fun, they never again wanted to be lazy or selfish.

Well, now you know something about Brownies and how they got their name. Next you will want to know what they are called in other countries, and why they are not all called Brownies.

The Brownie in this country is a happy good little fairy creature, but in some countries they have no good fairies, only wicked trolls or evil spirits. So the name 'Brownie' wouldn't mean anything to them at all.

Also in some countries the owl is thought to bring bad luck, so you couldn't tell them the story of the Wise Brown Owl, nor could you have the Brownie Guider called Brown Owl by the members of the Pack. Not all Brownie Guiders are called Brown Owl, but some Packs like to give her that name after the splendid Wise Brown Owl of the wood.

An Italian Brownie

So other countries found different names for the junior members of the Girl Guides, and they had to use other stories from their own folklore to explain the reason for their names and what they did.

In Switzerland they are called the *Petites Ailes* – Little Wings of Bees – and live in a *ruche* (hive). Their story tells how one day a cunning enemy entered the hive and said all sorts of wrong things to them. He told them it was much nicer to do nothing than to work; and why didn't they refuse to do as they were told because it was much more fun to do as they liked.

The Bees were very upset and didn't know what they should do, but then the good ones in the hive got together, and *working together* they drove out the enemy and his followers.

The picture on the left shows one of the Italian Brownies. They are called *Coccinelle* (Ladybirds) and *Primule* (Primula flowers). The *Coccinelle* wear red caps with black spots, like those on a ladybird's wings. There are seven black spots on these caps to remind them of their seven laws.

Pakistani Brownies are called Bluebirds, because a Bluebird brings happiness. The Leader of their Flock is the Wise Bird. In India they are Bulbuls. The Bulbuls are cheerful small birds who like to keep together in flocks, rather like our sparrows. So these Packs are also called Flocks.

Most Pakistani and Indian girls wear their hair long, so one of the skills a Bluebird or Bulbul learns is how to plait her own, or her sister's hair, neatly.

Most Brownies enjoy being out of doors, but Brownies in very hot countries are often glad to meet under the shade of trees or on a verandah because the sun is so hot.

So the Sunbeams of the Gilbert and Ellice Islands in the Pacific Ocean often meet at the village Maneabo, which is a meeting place with a thatched roof and open sides. In this shade it is cool enough to play games. Sunbeams love making things, just as all Brownies do, and they are very good at weaving mats and baskets from coconut fronds.

The Sixes of these Pacific Island Sunbeams are called Wind, Flames, Moonbeams, Stars, Raindrops, Waves, Rainbows and Clouds.

The Brownies of Swaziland are called Blue Jays. The Blue Jay is a Royal bird, and is one of the emblems used on the King's crown, and also in the Swaziland flag. It has beautiful blue wings, so the Blue Jays wear a blue uniform dress.

The Leader of a Flock of Blue Jays is called the Wise Bird. Each Flock is divided into nests, and each nest is named after a colour linked to a tree, so Blue nest would be in a Blue Gum tree, Yellow nest in a Yellow Wattle, and so on.

Greek Brownies are also named after birds. They are called *Poulia*, which means Little Birds.

A Dutch Brownie

Yes, Brownies have friends all over the world, and no matter what they are called, or what colour uniforms they wear, or where they meet, they are all alike because all have made a Promise to do their best and to help other people.

It is the Promise that really makes a Brownie.

A Promise is a very important thing to make, because once a promise is made it must be kept. Of course some promises have a very short life. There is the promise a girl may make to a teacher not to speak while she is out of the classroom – that is a short promise.

But the Promise a Brownie makes is one which will last the whole of her life, so she has to be quite sure she really understands what she is promising.

She will have been learning something about this Promise and some of the exciting things Brownies do, in the weeks she attends Pack Meetings, during which time she decides whether to be a Brownie, or not.

A new Brownie wears her uniform for the first time on the special day of her Promise Ceremony. And this is truly a 'special day', because it is the day she makes her Brownie Guide Promise, and receives her Brownie Guide Badge. You can see this ceremony in the picture on the left.

It is a special day for all the Pack, too, because every time a new Brownie makes her Promise, the other Brownies renew their Promise at the same time.

The new Brownie promises *to do her best* to keep this Promise, and all the time she is in the Pack she will learn more about how she can do this.

You notice a Brownie promises 'to do her best'. Just making a big Promise doesn't at once make a girl a perfect Brownie, but it does mean that she is going to try her hardest to work and play so that she will always be the very best she can possibly be, and not just when she is in uniform at a Brownie Meeting or other Brownie event, but every day, everywhere.

The first part of the Promise a Brownie makes is to 'do her duty to God'. There are many ways a Brownie can do this. She can go to a place of worship regularly to learn more about God and how He wants her to live. Then, just as a Brownie talks to her special friend and shares all the happy, the beautiful, and even the sad things in life with her, so she shares all these things with God as her extra-special friend – she does this through her prayers, when she talks with God.

*Brownies
leaving Church*

Because a Brownie is always on the look-out to help others, she also helps God by doing such useful things as collecting the books after a Service or perhaps helping with the dusting at Church. She may clean some of the brasses, or tend part of the Church garden.

Another way a Brownie does her duty to God is by being a cheerful person who tries not to grumble. A happy smiling Brownie makes those around her feel more cheerful. And a Brownie who gets on with any task cheerfully instead of grumbling and grousing about it is a really nice person to know.

Some Brownies are clever at writing things, so often a Brownie will write a Prayer for the Pack to use in their Pack Meeting. This may be a Thank You Prayer, or one asking God to help people who are in trouble.

A British Brownie also promises to 'serve the Queen'. A Brownie of another country makes the same promise, but to the head of her own country – King, Queen or President.

Our Queen once made a great promise herself. She promised she would spend her whole life helping and serving us, that is all the people in the countries over which she is head – the Commonwealth. But she knew this was going to be a hard promise to keep faithfully, so she asked everyone to help her and pray for her.

So a Brownie remembers the Queen's request and prays for her regularly, and she learns to understand the National Anthem which is also a prayer.

Other ways in which she serves her Queen are by obeying the safety rules of the road; keeping the country code which reminds people always to shut gates, not to damage hedges, not to let dogs run free among sheep, not to play in fields where crops are growing, etc. Another way she serves is by picking up litter, and never dropping any of her own, of course; and she is always most careful to obey the school crossing patrol person and the police.

The Queen has to meet and be friendly and helpful to many people who visit her, especially to people from other countries. So a Brownie can also serve the Queen by welcoming newcomers into her class at school, or into the Brownie Pack, especially anyone from another country to whom everything here would be strange.

New members of the pack are welcomed

A Brownie game

A Brownie is always on the look-out for ways in which she can help other people, especially those at home. But to be really helpful, a Brownie must first learn how to do jobs properly. If she doesn't, then instead of being a useful person, she would be nothing but a nuisance, just as Betty and Tommy were – at first – leaving behind nothing but a mess for someone else to clear up – usually Mother!

So a Brownie learns how to wash up properly, cleaning the sink after her. She learns to clean the bath and wash-basin after she has used them. Then she discovers how much nicer clothes look when they have been carefully ironed, and how lovely a well-polished table looks.

She is pleased when someone says how well she has cleaned her shoes, and thrilled when Daddy is delighted that a Brownie has been cleaning *his* shoes in secret.

Brownies also learn how to pack up parcels skilfully at Christmas and birthday times – so important when they have to go through our busy postal system.

A Brownie also discovers ways in which she can help to make her own home safe from accidents. She is careful not to leave knives lying about where a small brother or sister might get at them, and to keep a guard around a fire. And she does her best to remember never to leave her toys lying about on the floor where someone might fall over them.

She learns to cook, too. Not just potatoes and other vegetables, but exciting things like Fairy Cakes which she can then serve to guests at her own party, or a Brownie Party.

Yes, Brownies are very busy people, and because they are always so busy, they are happy. There are so many interesting things to do in life, and a Brownie is all the time discovering new and exciting things to do.

They enjoy making things, especially when the things they make are to be presents for others, such as book-markers, tea cosies, greeting cards, models, or toys for younger children. Because a Brownie wants to make things really well, she may learn how to knit and sew, and to use simple carpentry tools.

Brownies present a knitted patchwork blanket to the local hospital

Above all, Brownies like to be out-of-doors, exploring parks, gardens, and the countryside. It's fun to follow a trail, specially when the trail is laid by a Golden Goose who leaves yellow feathers for the Brownies to follow, and leads them at last to the buried treasure.

It's a thrill to watch a plant grow from a seed or bulb, and Brownies are very good at growing plants. They are also clever at making attractive miniature gardens, and many a person in hospital or sick at home has been given hours of pleasure by a gift of a garden in a dish.

Every Brownie likes collecting things, and there are so many interesting things she can collect. Sometimes these are outdoor things, like leaves, flowers, feathers, shells, stones; or they may be indoor things like stamps, postcards, postmarks.

To do the many interesting things a Brownie does, she needs to Keep Fit, she discovers how and why it is so important to keep her teeth, skin and hair clean. She learns to skip well, and to play dozens and dozens of games, some of them to help her Keep Fit, some to make her more wide-awake by challenging her to use her nose, her eyes, or her ears to the full.

Brownies play lots of games, sometimes in the Pack, sometimes in their Sixes, and sometimes on their own. It is surprising what a lot can be learnt through playing a game.

Often Brownies as a Pack have important matters to discuss and special Adventures, known as Brownie Ventures, to plan.

So then they go into Pow Wow, just as the Red Indians used to do when they discussed tribal matters.

The Pack sits in a ring, as close to one another as they can so that everyone can hear what is said, and everyone has a chance to give their ideas.

In Pow Wow the Pack may plan special Good Turns, such as a Carol Concert, or the making of knitted-square blankets, or arranging a concert to raise money to be spent on parcels for elderly people, or toys for children who get very few. Or they may plan a special Brownie Bazaar to get money to train a dog for a blind person, or to buy a special machine to help deaf children to learn to read and speak.

Quite often Good Turns become Brownie Ventures; it did for the Pack who decided to paint the gate for an elderly lady's garden – it led to their painting the whole garden fence! And for that they had to buy paint, and that meant raising money; and then they had to discover the right way to do such a big painting job, and for that fathers had to step in and show them.

Then another Pack thought it would be a good idea to collect old blankets, cut out the best parts, hem them round, and give them to the Animals' Hospital. This resulted in an invitation from the Vet-in-charge to visit the Hospital and see their blankets in use, and

before they knew where they were, they had become even busier and were working hard raising money to help the animals in need.

Brownie Revels at Framlingham Castle.
The theme, Olympic Games

Apart from all the things a Brownie does in her own Pack, there are even more thrilling days when she meets with neighbouring Packs at special Brownie Parties, called Revels.

But Revels aren't just an ordinary party – they do play games – lots of them – and have a special party tea, but above all a Brownie has to use her imagination and skill both before the Revels and at them, because every Revels becomes some Great Event for the day.

For instance one winter Revels which had to be held indoors, became a Super Circus. Each Pack dressed up as one Circus act, and then had to put on a suitable act to entertain the other Packs. So one Pack were clowns, and had to do a funny Clowns' act. Another Pack were acrobats, and had to do an acrobatic display. Yet another Pack were performing animals, and some splendid animals they became, too. Another Pack became a troupe of dancers.

On one occasion an outdoor Revels took a favourite story book as their idea – *The Wind in the Willows*. They became the animals in the story, wearing head-dresses to show who they were, having made these before the Revels. They played outdoor and nature games, and then set off to follow a special trail made by Moley's footsteps which eventually led them to the picnic area – Badger's house by the stream.

Another Revels became a big Pow Wow of Red Indian tribes, each Pack being a different tribe. Sometimes if Packs in very scattered areas meet together for Brownie Revels, it means that certain Brownies have to stay overnight. Then the Revels become an even greater Adventure, almost a Pack Holiday in fact!

Some Packs really do go away on a holiday together. This is the most exciting Brownie adventure of all. Just imagine spending a whole week with your Brownie friends in a special Brownie Pack Holiday Home; what a wonderful chance to put into practice all the skills you have learnt in Brownies. Skills like making scones and salads, frying sausages, preparing vegetables, making beds – not just ordinary beds, but camp beds, or perhaps bunk beds, one on top of the other, and usually with cute little ladders to climb up; cleaning windows, weeding flower-beds, not to mention the splendid games you can play in the big garden, the fields and the woods, and the storytimes you can have at night before going to bed in a big room with your friends.

Of course not every Pack is able to go away together for a whole week, so instead they have Pack Outings for a day at a time. Perhaps they may visit a Zoo, a large park, or have a day at the seaside. But whatever they decide to do, having talked about it first in Pow Wow, you can be sure it will be a thoroughly happy day for all.

In addition to Brownie Revels, Holidays and Outings, there is usually one day, perhaps more, in the year when a Brownie meets with other members of the big Movement to which she belongs – the Cub Scouts, Scouts, and Guides. This may be a big County Rally, or it may be a special Church Service, or some important happening in her own town.

A Brownie outing at Orford Castle

It's a great thrill to meet so many other members of the same Movement and to know that they have all made the same Promise as you.

Another day on which Brownies may meet other members of the Movement is Thinking Day.

Thinking Day is a special day in the year set aside for Brownies and Guides to think especially about themselves and other members of the Movement. The date is February 22nd, and Scouts call it 'Founders Day'. This date was chosen because it was the birthday of Lord Baden-Powell, and also that of his wife, Olave, Lady Baden-Powell, who became the Chief Guide of the World in 1930. Lady Baden-Powell died in 1977.

On this day Brownies often meet the Guide Company into which the Brownies can go some time between their tenth and eleventh birthdays. And at this Meeting they usually have a special Thinking Day Ceremony when they remember their Founder and say another 'thank you' for the splendid game of Scouting and Guiding he gave them. They also 'think' especially of their fellow Brownies and

Guides all over the world, pray for them, and wish them a Guiding 'Happy Birthday'.

But not only do they 'think' about them, they also 'do' something, because at these special Thinking Day Meetings everyone brings a small offering of money. This money is put into the Thinking Day Fund, and then used to help Packs and Companies all round the world – perhaps a Pack which has lost all its equipment, uniforms and badges in a disastrous flood; or to buy uniforms and badges for a new Pack in an orphanage or hospital.

It is fun for a Brownie to learn how to do new things which will help her to carry out her Promise. So a Brownie works for many badges.

The most important badge is her Brownie Guide Badge. This is the badge which is pinned on her tie the day she makes her Promise, and so becomes a full member of the Pack.

From then on a Brownie has so many interests to follow, and so many new things to do, she has no time to be bored. Not only does she explore new things to do at home, but she also discovers how to get the most enjoyment out of her hobbies, and often how to use them to give pleasure to others, too.

For instance, a Brownie who loves singing can work for her Singer Badge, and then use this new skill to sing in a concert to raise money to help equip another Animals' Hospital, or to buy a dinner for an elderly or needy person.

Or a Brownie who particularly enjoys collecting can perhaps make a large collection of shells in readiness for her Collector's Badge, and then one day she can give that collection, or one like it, to a child in hospital; maybe a child who has been in hospital a long, long time and has never seen the sea and all the wonderful animals that live in and by it.

Then a Brownie who likes making soft toys, or knitting, or sewing, can make many useful things in readiness for Toymaker, Knitter or Needleworker Badge. Many of the things she makes can then be used as presents, or to sell at a Pack Bazaar.

Brownies running a stall at a local bazaar

A Brownie making a cushion for her Needleworker Badge

The badges mentioned so far, and many more, are called Interest Badges, and a Brownie usually works for these alone, perhaps with some help from her Brownie Guider and parents.

But there are other badges a Brownie works towards the whole time she is in the Pack – the Brownie Journeys.

There are three Journeys – Footpath, Road and Highway, each with their own Challenges. Which Journey a Brownie will take will depend on her age, but every Brownie will try to complete the Highway Journey as this will help her to be ready to join the Guide Company.

When a Brownie is taking part in a Brownie Venture, she can wear a Venture Badge.

To help a Brownie while she is a member of the Pack are the adult Leaders, who are known as Brownie Guiders. Then she may have many other things, such as her own Brownie Guide Handbook packed full of hints and ideas for exciting things to do. Also there is a series of Pocket Books in which she can record all she has done as a Brownie: Pack Ventures, Interest Badges, Journey Challenges, and all the other interesting things she has done by herself or with her Pack.

A Brownie shows a new recruit the
Brownie Guide Handbook

And so comes the great day when a Brownie goes on to Guides.

She knows quite a lot about the Guide Company already through visiting their Meetings, perhaps meeting some of them at local events, or perhaps through her Pack Leader who is a Guide helping in the Brownie Pack.

Because as a Brownie she has been learning so many things, she is quite ready when she becomes a Guide to take part in the wider activities of a Guide Company, and to join in the exciting things they do; things such as camping, patrol hikes, camp fire singing, first aid and home nursing, map-reading, photography, bird watching, swimming, etc.

A Brownie will also discover that she can continue the hobbies she started on her Brownie Journey, but now she can learn even more about them.

Within a Brownie Pack a Brownie belongs to a small group called a Six. In the Guide Company these groups are called Patrols, and Guides do far more together, as a Patrol, than Brownies do as a Six.

A Brownie will also find she has another Motto to live up to. In Brownies her motto was 'Lend a Hand'. In Guides it will be 'Be Prepared'. This Motto is shared by all Guides and Scouts everywhere.

A Brownie Guider helps a group of Brownies to make a patchwork blanket

One wonders if Florence and Mabel would find Brownies as exciting today as they did when they became the first Rosebuds. Of course they would. In fact they'd find it far more exciting, because girls are allowed to do so much more now than they were at the beginning of the 20th century. Especially if they are Brownie Guides!

Books to help you

Here are some books to help you to become a good Brownie Guide by working for your interest badges.

 Woodworker
Woodwork
(Learnabout)

 Knitter
Knitting
(Learnabout)

 Collector
Leaves (Leader)
Stamp Collecting
(Learnabout)
Coin Collecting (Learnabout)

 Needleworker
Sewing
(Learnabout)

 Discoverer
British Wild
Animals (Nature)
British Wild
Flowers (Nature)

 Toymaker
Toys and Games
to make
(Hobbies)
Sewing (Learnabout)
Knitting (Learnabout)

 Animal Lover
Pets
(Learnabout)

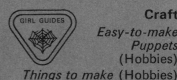 **Craft**
Easy-to-make
Puppets
(Hobbies)
Things to make (Hobbies)
More things to make
(Hobbies)
Sewing (Learnabout)
Knitting (Learnabout)
Crochet (Learnabout)

Gardener
Indoor
Gardening
(Learnabout)
Garden Flowers (Nature)